SANDWELL
LIBRARIES

Cal's Log

WRITTEN BY
ANTHONY

D1385976

ILLUSTRATED BY MARK OLDROYD

12565385

ONE

The sea was flat calm with a strange glow.

'I've never seen weather like this before,' said Anna.

Mac didn't answer, staring out at the gleam on the horizon. He was stocky, with red hair, while his cousin was tall and dark.

Mac and Anna were both twelve years old and had known each other for a long time. They often knew what each other was thinking.

That day the forecast had been good – light winds and clear conditions – unusual for Shetland, which was famous for its storms and choppy seas. But there was always a lingering doubt. Bad weather could blow up fast here.

Mac and Anna were very experienced sailors, and for many years had sailed their much-loved dinghy, *Puffin*. But this summer there had been so many days of lashing winds and rip tides that they had hardly sailed her at all.

Mac knew the forecast was usually fairly accurate. All we're seeing is some weird light, he told himself. They couldn't be put off by that!

Mac and Anna had already hauled up *Puffin's* sails, which were fluttering gently in the lee of the harbour wall.

The fishing fleet had long since put to sea and Anna's father's craft shop was closed for lunch. No adults were available, thought Mac. His parents were out; his father examining the salmon cages on the family fish farm and his mother striding the sands with the dogs. He and Anna had to make their own decisions.

Anna's parents had come up from London five years ago to get out of the 'rat race'. Mac, who had lived in Shetland all his life, had never been to London.

'We'll go,' he said abruptly, and Anna nodded far too casually. As he spoke, Mac realized he had made a decision that went against his better judgment. But now he had made it, he didn't want to back down. Besides, they weren't going to sea for that long…

'You're the local man,' said Anna, grinning up at him from her place at the helm.

Anna, however, felt uneasy. Even though she was usually bossy, she felt she didn't want to interfere this time. She didn't want Mac thinking she was a spoilsport.

Mac was still worried by the strange glow in the sky but he wasn't going to show Anna that he was a coward.

He cast off and Anna, at the helm, steered them out of the harbour, handling the mainsail with her usual easy touch.

Puffin began to bound forward on playful waves, but when Mac looked up he could see the sea birds heading for their roosts in the cliffs. That's odd, he thought.

Mac looked out towards the stack. The glow had spread slightly as a kind of purple haze. But there was only a moderate breeze. We're going to be fine, he thought. There won't be any problems.

TWO

Puffin was heading towards Sharp's Stack, a huge rock that reared out of the sea, a couple of miles offshore. Mac and Anna's plan had been to sail round the stack and then make for home. It was one of their favourite trips. Usually the voyage only took a couple of hours, and they were both sure that *Puffin* would be back at her mooring in the harbour by five.

They had often made up stories about the rock, which looked like a massive castle looming out of the grey-green sea. Its sheer dark sides reached up out of the waves which boiled around the base. None of the locals would sail anywhere near it. But Mac and Anna enjoyed the challenge of sailing around the stack.

The top was hundreds of metres high, and when the wind whistled amongst its craggy weathered surface there was a strange sound, as if a flute was being played in some great baronial hall in the rock.

The stack was meant to be haunted by

the souls of shipwrecked mariners who appeared as seals on the surrounding rocks. There were quite a few of them now, black shapes in the swell.

'What *is* that glow?' asked Anna as if she were trying to get Mac to give in and go back.

Mac felt even more uneasy.

'The end of the world,' he told her, making a feeble attempt at a joke.

Anna was usually calm, unflappable, but she, too, was tense. It'll be all right, she told herself. There's no need to worry. No need to say anything.

The stack rose out of the sea in front of them, its black sides shining as the waves crashed relentlessly against it.

'Nasty currents out there today,' said Anna. 'Let's not go as close to the stack as we usually do.'

The sun, a pale swollen orange, broke through the clouds, and the wind lessened.

Puffin sailed on for another ten minutes. Mac and Anna sat in silence, sweating underneath their life-jackets and sweaters.

'It's not Shetland weather,' said Mac.

There was still only a hint of wind, an occasional breeze that made the waves slap against the *Puffin's* bows.

'Are we still going round the stack?' asked Anna.

Mac was surprised at her hesitation. 'We'll give it a wider berth than usual. Anyway, there's quite a swell running.'

Why couldn't they admit their fears to each other and sail for home?

Sharp's Stack was looming up in front of them now, and the dull sound of thunder in the distance made Mac realize that the time had come to put a stop to all this hesitation.

'Let's go about. It's time to turn back,' he said.

At last Anna felt a sense of overpowering relief. She had never seen the stack looking so evil. The weather had made the decision for them. They were going to be all right now.

'Ready about,' she said quietly as they both ducked under the boom.

The thunder rumbled again and then the wind came, at first a series of thrusting gusts and then more steadily, whipping up the wave crests.

'That was quick,' said Anna.

'Freak weather,' Mac muttered.

'The glow –'

'It wasn't forecast.'

Mac felt the fear creeping over him. Had they left it too late?

A few moments later the glow disappeared and the sky turned black. The storm broke overhead with a thunderclap so loud that it resounded in their ears. The waves suddenly seemed much bigger. The weather had turned in seconds.

Panic flooded Mac's mind. They had put to sea without thinking properly, and now they were going to pay.

Anna, at the helm, tried to aim for the harbour, but the current had taken them too far over and the tide was against them. They weren't going to make it.

Panic had gripped them both now. The gusts began to get harder, more vicious.

The waves gripped *Puffin*, spinning her round, forcing the dinghy to head into the wind.

Then they heard a cracking sound and realized that the mast had snapped.

Mac ducked as the rigging, sails and bits of splintered timber rained down on him, but fortunately most of it went overboard and only a small amount of water slopped on board.

Anna, still at the helm but half-covered in sail, watched helplessly as *Puffin* drifted towards the stack. There was nothing that either of them could do – absolutely nothing. She felt numbed and horrified. The dinghy was being drawn towards the place she was most frightened of. In fact, it was as if the stack had already got the *Puffin* in its power and was trawling them in like captured fish.

Mac cut away the remainder of the rigging and gazed up at Anna, realizing she was just as afraid as he was.

'Look, there are caves in the stack,' he said wildly.

'Do you think we could land there?'

'We don't have any choice about where we're going.'

Sharp's Stack reared out of the waves, spray rising more than half-way up its sheer black sides, while the sky above was a purple black, lit by forked lightning. Then the rain came, a total downpour as if some dam in the sky had burst.

'We're going to be hit by that wave,' yelled Mac and they watched in

unbelieving horror as the wall of water
roared towards them.

What have you learnt about the characters of
Mac and Anna so far?

THREE

Puffin rose up, hovered on the brink of the wave and then capsized, throwing them out into the lashing sea.

Gasping with cold and shock, Mac and Anna desperately tried to swim, but the waves were so high that it was more like being propelled up a mountain and down the other side at an uncontrollable speed.

Anna, now on a crest, saw she was being swept towards the stack. A strong current was pulling her towards a dark cave mouth. This had to be the end. In seconds they would both be dashed up against the black, barnacle-encrusted rock.

'Keep down!' Anna shouted to Mac. 'You've got to keep down.' She had just noticed a gap between the roof of the cave and the waves. If they kept their heads low they might just be swept inside. The possibility was slim but it was the only chance they had.

The current slowed, creating a patch of slack water. With the strange feeling of being sucked in, Anna swam as hard as she could past the weed-draped rocks, fighting her way towards the cave.

Then she dived beneath the surface, and when she came up again, Anna found herself in the cave, heading towards a low flat ledge. The current was beginning to pick up speed again, and Anna had to stop herself being swept along with it.

'Get out on the ledge,' she bellowed, hoping that Mac was following. 'You've got to get out.'

Fortunately Mac had also dived, but when he came up again he had bumped his head on the roof of the cave. Nevertheless, he heard Anna's command above the booming sound of the sea. Then he saw her half-standing in shallow water, one hand outstretched.

But Mac could not stop. The current swept him past Anna. He grasped an overhang, tearing his hands on the rough barnacles, but managing to hold on.

Then he saw Anna standing above him. She crouched down.

'Grab my hands,' she shouted, trying to steady herself on the slippery ledge.

'I'll only pull you back in.'

'Do as I say!'

Mac realized that he couldn't cling on much longer. The tide was tugging at him and he would soon be swept away. Panicking, he tried to summon up the strength to heave himself up.

With a cry of fear, Mac reached up and Anna grabbed his wrists.

'Come on,' she yelled. 'I've got you.'

With a tremendous effort he pushed himself up until his stomach was painfully sliding over sharp, craggy rock.

Once they were safe, they both lay on the rock ledge, gasping.

Slowly and painfully they both began to realize the danger they were still in. The stack had captured them and they were not going to escape that easily.

Mac and Anna could hear the thundering of the storm outside. They might have found temporary shelter but they were also imprisoned.

Then Mac remembered the survival kit he always kept in waterproof packets in his life-jacket pockets.

Assembling it had always seemed like a game to him. Now he was going to have to use the kit for real.

Mac pulled out a waterproof torch. Then he checked over the rest of the stuff: a first aid kit, a multi-purpose knife, mint cake, a packet of fire-lighters and matches, spare batteries for the torch and a distress flare.

He shone the beam slowly around the wall of the cave. There was something wrong.

'What's the matter?' Anna asked, seeing the look in his eyes.

'The tide comes right up to the roof of the cave. See that mark on the wall.'

Even as he spoke they could see the water splashing on to the ledge.

Mac flashed the torch over the seaweed-hung wall again and noticed a dark space at the back. They both got up and stumbled towards it.

'It's a sort of chimney,' he said with relief. 'A long slit in the rock. But it might not lead to the top of the stack. It could be a dead end.'

'We could climb up through it,' said Anna. 'If we braced ourselves against the walls, maybe we could lever ourselves up. It's narrow enough.'

Mac nodded. Anna was right. 'You done any climbing?'

'No. But I saw this TV programme about one of these chimneys. You press yourself against the back wall and push against the front with your feet.'

'I'll go first,' said Mac, 'I'm shorter. If I can brace myself against the walls, then so can you.'

He took off his life-jacket and Anna did the same, dumping them down on the ledge. Then he shoved his survival kit into the zip pockets of his cords.

'We're going to get out of this. If we can make it to the top of the stack, someone's bound to see us.'

'But we can't be sure the gap goes all the way up.'

Mac switched off the torch and stared up into the darkness, determined to be optimistic. 'Isn't that a patch of light up there?'

Anna gazed up eagerly, but all she could see was a slightly greyer blackness.

'Come on then.' Mac hoisted himself up into the first crevice in the chimney and braced his back against the wall.

As he worked his way slowly up, he began to feel more secure, despite the fact that his sodden clothes were clinging to him and his muscles began to feel stretched and sore.

'How are you doing?' Mac bellowed down the narrow shaft.

'OK.' Anna's voice was thin and distant.

Mac paused and looked down. Below her was the white curl of the tide that had already covered their ledge. There was no way back.

How do you think Mac and Anna felt, once they were inside the stack?

FOUR

Despite torn and bleeding fingers, Anna and Mac struggled on up, their situation made slightly easier by the fact that the shaft was getting narrower and there seemed to be rather more rocky projections than there had been lower down.

Anna, whose long legs and arms gave her an advantage, soon found that the pain was decreasing and she was climbing faster, easily catching up with Mac.

Mac had slowed up now, occasionally dragging out his torch and swinging the beam around the walls of the chimney.

'Wait,' said Anna suddenly. 'It's getting wider.'

Mac nodded. 'Only a bit. I think we can still brace ourselves.'

But a few minutes later he lost his footing, and with a warning cry began to slide down towards her.

Anna looked up and screamed in terror. Just as she had feared, he was going to take her with him into the swirling sea below.

Then Mac managed to jam his arms

and legs again and came to a shuddering halt.

She heard him sob in the darkness and called up, 'You all right?'

'I was wrong. The chimney does widen out.' His voice was thin and hopeless. 'We're trapped. We can't go up or down.'

'But we might be able to go *inside*,' said Anna quietly.

'What are you on about?'

'Didn't you see that big crevice in the rock? We'd have to squeeze in but there's a chance it might turn out to be a tunnel. Shine your torch on the opposite wall of the chimney as we go back down.'

Bracing themselves against the walls, they inched down painfully. Their legs and arms ached horribly, and holding the torch made Mac's progress even more difficult.

Suddenly he saw the narrow slit and realized they might just be able to squeeze into it. Pressing himself even harder against the opposite wall, Mac put a foot and then a hand into the slit, feeling a ridge of rock. He pulled and was suddenly inside.

With a mixture of relief and anxiety, he saw that the crevice seemed to stretch back some way and was on one level.

Mac turned back and shone the torch so that Anna could scramble in behind him. She looked drained and exhausted.

'You OK?'

'Just a bit tired.'

'So am I. Do you want something to eat? I've got mint cake. It's probably a bit squashed after climbing up the chimney.'

They walked on, closed in by the walls on either side of them. Suppose they came to a dead end? What then?

'Has this stack ever been explored before?' she asked.

'I'm sure it hasn't. It's too difficult to get into – as we found out.' Mac paused. 'I reckon we could be the first people here in centuries.'

I am alone. Fergus and Angus died when the chimney widened. They insisted on continuing, despite all my appeals. I am writing by candlelight, having witnessed their bodies hurtle into the waves.

Because I am alone I intend to write my journal in the ship's log I rescued from the *Petrel*. I will also try to map these tunnels. I am determined to escape.

I am now the only survivor.

The storm was the worst I have ever known. There were strange lights in the sky and a hurricane that seemed to blow from hell. The fierce wind and the driving storm broke our mast and we drifted for a day before being wrecked on the stack.

I am fourteen years old. My name is Cal and I was the ship's cabin boy. My two companions were older members of the crew. The others drowned. God rest their souls.

The three of us fought the currents and found shelter. But we soon realized we were in a trap, for the tide mark on the walls showed the cave was submerged at high tide. We had to climb for our lives.

I have a candle and a tinder-box in my oilskin bag which also contains the log, my silver pencil, a few ship's biscuits and a flask of water.

If only I had a companion.

I have to get to the top of the stack. Surely I'll be

seen from such a vantage point? But *how* will they rescue me? Could they send a boat across on a calm day? Maybe I could climb down. If not, there might be a point from which I could jump into the sea. They could pick me up from there – if I survive. But *will* they come?

It pains me so much to think of home, but the visions are with me at all times. The twins are in the orchard, Grandmother is reading in the drawing room, my father is at his desk, my mother is arguing with Cook. These pictures are as painful as the cuts in my hands from grasping the jagged rock.

One day I'd hoped to run my father's ships with as much patience and expertise as he has achieved over the years. But if I die he will have no heir. And then what will happen to Patterson and Whitgift? The Whitgift line died out years ago. Only the Pattersons are left – my father and I.

I can see Father looking down at the fleet as we loaded at the quayside. Looking down with pride and love.

My father told me I was to sail with every ship, learn every rope, work alongside the crew before I could take my place beside him. I was to learn with humility, take the roughest of duties.

My father had been cabin boy before me and his father before him. It is a family tradition for the heir to go before the mast, to endure every hardship.

This was my first ship and it was a hard passage. I learned to fight with my fists, to drink rum and to climb the mast to the crows nest, despite my fear of heights. I learned to scrub decks. I understood how it felt to have scurvy.

I had been on board the *Petrel* for four months before she foundered in the storm, and during that time, I hope I had passed some of the tests at least, although there would have been many more to come. To my joy I had overheard the mate say, 'That young Cal's cast in the same mould as his father. He'll do.'

He'll do? The words still bring tears to my

eyes, especially when I look into the darkness of this tunnel. Will I escape or will my father be the last of us?

The stack is my final test.

I see Emily and Jane running through the long grass under the apple trees towards me, their hands outstretched, Mrs Smiley, their governess, with a basket of books, watching. They've been learning their lessons under the trees and I can see there is plum juice on their mouths from raiding the lower branches. Their hands are probably sticky with it, too. They call my name.

But there is no answer.

I'm in the stack.

Will you come looking for me, Father?

I shall begin to walk again, now I'm rested. I may have much more to endure. Please God, keep me safe. I shall scratch arrows on the wall with my knife and make my map so that I'll know if I have been walking in a circle.

Do you think the arrows will show Mac and Anna the way out?

FIVE

'What's this?' asked Mac as he moved on down the tunnel, his torch beam sweeping the rocky walls. 'Who says no one's been down here before?'

They both paused in surprise.

'That arrow looks as if it was carved in the rock a long time ago,' said Anna.

'It means there's a way out. All we have to do is to follow the arrows.'

'Who says they're going anywhere?'

But he was not to be put off. 'I reckon they'll lead to the top. Or at least to somewhere we can attract attention.' He paused, glancing back at her. 'What's the matter?'

'Nothing,' Anna said bitterly. 'Nothing much. I mean – we're stuck out on a huge rock in the Atlantic with nothing to eat and nothing to drink, the *Puffin* wrecked and –'

Mac winced. 'It was my fault,' he began.

'Stop it!' Anna yelled.

'Stop what?' Mac looked at her uneasily. 'It was both our faults.'

They stumbled on for about ten minutes with the torch beam flashing ahead of them. Anna began to wonder if they should economize with the batteries and try and walk in the darkness. She knew Mac had his spares but how long would even these last as they wound their way round inside the hollow stack?

The arrows continued at regular intervals and that kept up Mac's spirits. Anna, however, had less faith in the arrows and she couldn't believe they were pointing to an exit.

'Another arrow,' said Mac with infuriating cheerfulness. 'The tunnel's going uphill now and getting a bit of a squeeze.'

'It certainly is,' Anna agreed miserably.

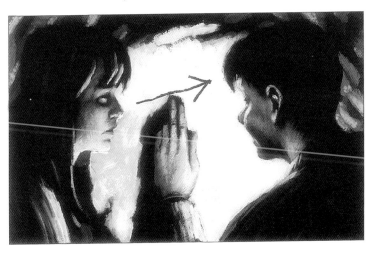

The walls are suffocating me as they become increasingly narrow, and sometimes, when I brush against them, they seem to be soft. Of course, I put this down to my fevered imagination. Despite my wet clothing and the cold dampness here, I'm beginning to sweat and I know I cannot bear much more. I'm still carving my arrows and drawing my map, despite the fact that the tunnel has not divided. Perhaps some time in the future other shipwrecked mariners will arrive in this terrible place and need my guidance.

My father's voice rings in my ears. 'The family business – it's everything to me. We have responsibilities to our employees. Do you know how many there are? Over four hundred. They'll starve without us, Cal. You'll never let me down, will you? I have to trust you with their future.'

You must trust me, Father. You must trust me to find a way out of this maze. I'll not let you down. I promise…

Half an hour has passed. The tunnel is going uphill and is much steeper. Even though I am lean I am finding that squeezing through its narrow walls is near impossible. But I will not give up.

Now, as I squeeze my way through the rock, I fancy I hear the sound of many footsteps behind me as I lead my shipwrecked mariners to safety.

I carve my arrows with pride.

'Can you make it?' asked Anna.

Squeezing himself through the rock made Mac feel as if he were suffocating. Light clouds of dust rained on him and he felt something flutter softly against his cheek. He gave a yelp of fear and came to a trembling halt, dropping the torch, which immediately went out.

Anna blundered into him in the pitch dark and Mac stuttered out, 'I – I've dropped the torch.'

'I can see that, though actually I can't see a thing.' She began to laugh wildly, more out of fear than anything else. Anna tried to stop, but the more she tried the more she laughed until her stomach hurt.

'Why don't you shut up?' yelled Mac, down on all fours now, trying to find the torch, but not having any success. 'Why don't you just *shut up*?'

But she couldn't. Anna's laughter echoed in the narrow space until it became shrill and ugly. She listened to the horrible sound for some time until she realized that it was coming from her. She managed to stop, feeling ashamed and stupid.

With a grunt of satisfaction, Mac found the torch at last. He had been desperately worried that it might be broken, but when he snapped it on again the beam shone as strongly as before.

Then he rose to his feet and shone the beam in Anna's direction. She was on the verge of tears.

'I'm sorry,' she said. 'I'm really sorry.'

Mac grinned at her, feeling much calmer now, and then swung the torch beam around the walls to find the next arrow.

'There you are,' he said. 'We're still on the trail.'

Now he felt almost hysterical himself, but with joy and the certainty that they were being led to safety. He'd been such a fool, getting worked up about the narrow tunnel, and the soft mouse-like thing that had touched him was probably a bat. So the stack wasn't lifeless after all. Rather than making him afraid, the existence of a bat colony made Mac feel he wasn't alone.

He continued to stumble on. The walls of the tunnel were now widening a little and the ground was rising much more sharply. But Mac was sure he could smell the sea. How could that be? They'd been going up rather than down.

'There's a light ahead,' he shouted suddenly. For the first time Mac glanced down at his watch and noticed it was just after six. They had been trapped in the stack for over two hours but it had seemed like as many days.

Anna had now developed a blister on her heel that was throbbing painfully. But the pale-grey light ahead of her was the most hopeful sign she had seen since they had been forced into this terrible fortress.

The walls of the tunnel were now about a metre apart, making progress much more possible, and the floor was getting increasingly steeper. As the light grew stronger, Anna's hopes soared.

She watched Mac begin a staggering run towards the end of the tunnel. Then he seemed to freeze. Despite her blister, Anna pushed herself on as hard as she could and joined Mac on the ledge.

Peering down, they both gazed into a sea-filled bottomless gorge.

The sea looked as trapped as they were, heaving in deadly confusion. The stack was hollow, thought Anna, and they had arrived at its centre, where this boiling pit had formed. Centuries of erosion must be the cause. They were surrounded by high rocky walls from which no bird flew or perched or sang.

Anna was terrified by the heaving surf that ground against the rocks, making a booming sound. Then she realized that this was where the current in the cave must

have been heading: right into the centre of the stack. But where did it come out?

Mac stared at the rock face intently and noticed another ragged tear but this time at sea level. 'It's like a blow hole. The water's being sucked out again under that rock. We'll have to go back,' he admitted miserably. 'The arrows were wrong.'

'Not wrong. Just hopeful,' said Anna shrewdly. 'Maybe whoever came this way before was carving the arrows as their trail. Maybe they weren't meant to indicate a definite route at all.'

They stared at each other in silence.

The purple storm clouds had gone, replaced by a slate grey overcast sky, the clouds broken here and there by streaks of pale sunlight.

The booming of the waves in the pit and the sheer rocky sides that surrounded them was an incredibly depressing sight.

'Wait a minute!' said Anna. 'Look at this.'

The scratchings were very faint on the wall behind them, and took time to decipher. But eventually they read the message: LOOK TO YOUR LEFT.

SIX

As I stood regarding the pit of hell, my spirits sank so low that I almost threw myself into its depths. I've never experienced such despair. After so long in the dark I arrived to find this infernal place.

At least I have mapped my journey, and my experience with the *Petrel's* charts has helped me to be more complete than I was.

'You'll never let me down, will you?' My father's words repeated again and again in my mind. I don't want to disobey him. I don't want to die. But what am I to do? What *can* I do? Go back down the tunnel? Or try the ledge out here? Could it lead somewhere? How am I to keep my balance? One false move and I'll plunge into the pit and be swallowed up. But Father would expect me to try.

The narrow ledge was a terrible experience but somehow I conquered its dangers. Several times I almost slipped and was sure that my last moment had come. Looking down at the pit I knew I could not continue. Then I heard my father's voice again. 'You'll never let me down, will you?' It echoed in my head and became louder than the roaring of the trapped waves below me. Because of his dear words I found the courage to reach another break in the rock, which I think may afford a passage.

I have indicated the ledge by scratching a message to those that may come behind me, God bless them. I am so tired and hungry and there is no light. But I must go into the darkness again.

'What does LOOK TO YOUR LEFT *mean*?' demanded Anna. 'There's just that narrow ledge.'

'That's what it *does* mean,' replied Mac shakily. 'What's more, there's another arrow.'

'It's all a con,' muttered Anna.

'It's our only hope.'

The ledge was narrow and damp, the rock smooth and dangerously slippery. If either of them took a wrong step, they would plunge down into the surf. Either they would be dashed to pieces on the rocks they could now see under the water, or they would be sucked through the blow hole.

Even if they *did* make it, there was no guarantee they would find an escape route, and another tunnel might just lead them back into the centre.

The dangers blazed in Mac and Anna's minds as they gazed down at the surging swell and the slippery ledge.

'I'll go and check it out,' said Mac. 'I still believe in the arrows even if you don't.'

'Then you're a fool,' she replied bluntly.

But he was already moving away from her and she grabbed his wrist and sharply pulled him back.

'Mac, don't go,' she yelled.

'You idiot!' he shouted back. 'You almost had me over.'

'Let's go back into the other tunnel. We may have missed something.' Anna's voice shook.

'No chance.'

'Please, Mac. If you fall into that awful pit, I'll be alone.'

Mac was angry and unable to make any decisions at all. He had never felt so afraid in his life and his mouth was now so dry he just couldn't argue with Anna any more.

'You *can't* leave me here, Mac. I can't stay here on my own.'

'Anna, it's now or we stay in this stack for ever.'

Anna made up her mind. 'I'm coming with you.'

Mac took another glance down and wished he hadn't. The waves lashed violently, overlapping each other in their frenzy.

'Wait a minute –' began Mac.

'We can't wait. We have to do it now. Just like you said.' Anna was already clambering over a large rock to the ledge.

What do we learn about Cal's character from his log?

SEVEN

The surface was much more slippery than even she had imagined. As a result Anna decided to inch along with her face pressed against the wall. But this made her feel even more unstable, as if some force from the pit was dragging her back.

Mac also hugged the rock, moving even more slowly than Anna, muttering and praying with each step. Suppose there wasn't another tunnel? Suppose they had to make a dreadful return journey over the ledge? The very thought of it terrified him.

Mac screamed as he suddenly lost his footing, but he managed to hang on to one of the few rocky projections. For a while he stayed where he was, rigid, frozen to the spot.

'Are you all right?' came Anna's voice in desperate appeal.

He couldn't reply, as if by taking breath the effort would hurtle him backwards into the pit.

'You've *got* to speak to me, Mac. Are you OK?'

In the end he managed a mumbled reply, but he still couldn't move.

'I can see a break in the rock,' said Anna, her voice rising with excitement. 'It's just a few metres along. I'm heading for it now.'

Mac still couldn't move.

'We're going to be all right,' she tried to reassure him.

'I'm there!' shouted Anna.

Mac froze for the second time. He felt like giving up, letting go. He *had* to let go. He couldn't go on clinging to this wet rock any longer. It would be so good to stop concentrating. To lose all sense of –

'Come on,' said Anna gently. 'You're doing brilliantly. There are only another few metres to go. I would say about six steps. Why don't I count you in?'

'No,' he muttered.

'Take your first step now,' she commanded.

Reluctantly Mac slid his foot along the ledge.

'Well done,' came the commanding voice he was beginning to hate. 'That's one – and now that's two. You'll soon be there.

Three and four. Brilliant! Only two more steps to go. Keep moving and I'll grab you. Let's go for a five and now a six, and I've got you –'

Mac screamed as he toppled backwards towards the pit. His mind whirled. This was it. He was going to die.

But Anna managed to reach out and grab him and she pulled him into the cave. He lay there for a while, unable to believe that he was safe and the ordeal was over.

'Thanks,' he said after a long silence. 'I'd have gone over if it hadn't been for you.'

'It's so awful here,' said Anna quietly, as if she had used up the last of her strength trying to coax Mac into the cave.

'It is, but I've got this strange feeling that someone's with us, that we've got a guide.'

'How do you mean?' quizzed Anna.

But Mac didn't know how to continue. 'It's just a feeling I've got.'

Mac unzipped his pocket and dragged out the torch, swinging the beam round the inside of the cave. To one side he saw a number of upside-down bats hanging in a row. Hurriedly he swept the other side wall with light, hoping not to disturb them but not really caring if he did. At least they were alive – just like him and Anna.

I have been wandering the darkness for what seems like days now. I have seen no natural light and I'm becoming weaker by the hour. Here at the rock wall I've tried to finish the map, but the darkness has been like a cloak and I am unable to tell if anyone could understand what I have drawn.

The stack is hollow and in its centre there is a giant pit from hell. I clung to the slippery ledge and became lost in the tunnels again. It is as if the devil created a rock and then made the inside into a giant honeycomb.

I shall try to sleep. My water bottle is empty, and although I found what I hoped was a rain pool, it tasted salty. Nevertheless I drank my fill. But now my throat is drier than ever. I can see the twins running towards me in the orchard. I take their hands, still sticky with plum juice.

If anyone finds me and they are also lost, I beg of you to be braver than me. Keep going. There must be a way out.

Please help me, Father.

What do you think Mac means when he says, 'we've got a guide'?

EIGHT

Mac and Anna rested and then ate some mint cake, which tasted delicious. But almost immediately they felt extremely thirsty and soon their mouths were horribly dry again.

'I'm going back to the ledge,' said Anna. 'There may be some rain-water out there.'

'You can't.' Mac was insistent.

'Why not? We're not going to find water in here.'

'Let me have the torch for a minute, then.' Anna swept the beam around the walls of the cave and suddenly Mac gave a cry of delight.

'What's that, then?'

There was a damp stain on the wall and he could see drops glistening on the rock. He got stiffly to his feet and examined the droplets carefully, seeing they had formed a small pool in a cleft of the rock.

He tasted the water cautiously while Anna watched him in silence, keeping Mac in the beam.

'It's rain seeping down the wall,' he said with satisfaction. 'And the pool's deep. Here – come and try it.'

They both cupped their hands and drank long and hard. The water was cold and deeply refreshing.

When they had drunk for what seemed a very long time, Mac said, 'There is hope. Even if we didn't think so. Let's push on and follow the arrows.'

Anna nodded. They had to reach a point where they could be seen, either on a higher ledge overlooking the coastline or, preferably, on top of the stack itself. Walking on into the cave they realized they were approaching another tunnel.

I have lost count of the days I have been here. All I do is think of food and that is the greatest torture of all.

I keep thinking of the Christmas lunch my father would serve for the staff in the covered dock. Long tables spread with white cloths and the ship's crew making a feast of the goose and the turkey, the chicken and the lamb, and if that is not enough, there is a haunch of venison and a pig on a spit. My father would feed over four hundred that day – the captains, the mates, the crews and all their families. I keep thinking of the crackling on the pork.

Now I am getting sleepy and the writing of this log is more difficult. I must conserve my strength, for I must study my map again and make sure it is as clear as it can be for others. I must be of service. I must honour my responsibilities. Father is telling me to do my duty.

This is where I may die. Dear Father, I pray you will never know what I have been through and just remember me as I was.

I love you and Mother and the twins more than anyone on this earth. I am sorry to have failed. I am sorry that I cannot take on the business. I know I have let you down. But I have done my best. And, in truth, I can do no more than be a guide. I hope I shall be needed.

Checking the map has weakened me still further but I think it is clear enough. What I have tried to do is to indicate the possible escape route as accurately as I can. I pray that I do not mislead. There must be a way out. I wish to God I had strength for further exploration. Perhaps the ground will continue to climb. Perhaps the tunnel will link with another chimney that will reach the top of the stack.

I pray to God that there is a way out for those who might have so faithfully followed my directions. I fear, however, that they must have cursed me many times for a fool. Perhaps this is my chance to redeem myself.

The map is in my log and my log is wrapped in oilcloth. I will keep it here in my hand.

I see shadows in the darkness. Could they be those who follow, those I lead? Or are they dream phantoms, the spirits of the stack come to claim me? Or is it the Grim Reaper, the Angel of Death himself?

If you discover my corpse tell my father about me and what has happened. His address is also in the log. Honour my name, I beg you.

Dear Father and Mother, I fear I must leave you soon. I'm so tired but I'm warm and comfortable although the fever has me in its grip. Too hot. Sometimes cold. Drowsy. Full of love for you. I can see us all now, walking to church on a bright spring Sunday, the river flowing beside us. I see ships in the harbour. Our ships.

Your obedient and ever loving son, Cal.

NINE

Mac and Anna had been walking in the tunnel for about twenty minutes, with the ground still rising and their spirits at their highest since they had entered the stack.

'You thinking what I'm thinking?' he asked suddenly.

'What's that?'

'Food.'

'We can have some more mint cake.'

'I'm sick of the taste of it. I've been thinking about a double cheeseburger and chips.'

'With lots of relish,' she added.

'And tomato sauce. Masses of tomato sauce. Bottles of it.'

They walked on in silence, each preoccupied with their own thoughts.

'The ground seems to have flattened out,' said Mac.

'Maybe we're near the top of the stack.' Anna was optimistic. 'Surely we'll come out into daylight soon?'

They were silent again, but it was no longer comfortable. As they rounded a sharp bend the ground began to rise again, but their relief was short-lived as Anna came to a stumbling halt.

'What have we stopped for?'

'We can't go on.'

'What do you mean?' he demanded, needing to misunderstand her. 'You tired or something? Come on – the tunnel must bend away to the right.'

'It would be nice if it did,' Anna replied quietly.

'I don't get you.' But Mac was still pretending to himself. Of course he knew what she meant. They had arrived at a dead end.

They both pushed at the rock with their hands, realizing at the same time how stupid they were being. There could be no possible doubt – there was no way forward. They had followed the arrows, only to be made fools of again. Now, even Mac was furious with their unknown guide.

'He's playing games,' he muttered.

'Why "he"?'

'I don't know. I just get this feeling he was a he. I could wring his neck,' said Mac as he flashed the torchlight around in growing panic. But there was quite clearly no way out.

Anna was silent as she gazed down at the floor. 'I don't think you need to bother about wringing his neck.'

'What do you mean?'

'It's too late.' She handed him the torch. 'Look.'

The beam picked out a skeleton that was not much bigger than Mac. The bones were white and delicate, gleaming back at them.

Mac's hand began to shake and when he glanced at Anna he could see that she was as deeply shocked as he was.

'The arrows –' She faltered. 'He made them.'

'I could feel him there. In that cave by the ledge. He's been guiding us.'

'To a dead end,' she muttered.

'Look – he's holding something. I think it's wrapped in oilcloth.' He paused. 'Shall I take a look?'

'Yes,' replied Anna in a small, tight voice. 'I think you should.'

Still Mac hesitated. Then with sudden

decision he reached down and gently removed the object. A little dust flew up and the skeleton hand rattled back on to the floor.

Mac's hands were still trembling violently and Anna could hardly bear to watch him trying to unwrap the parcel.

At last he succeeded and held up a small, leather book. Slowly, gently, Mac leafed through the pages. 'This is a ship's log – but used as a diary. It's in pretty good condition.'

'Let's move somewhere else,' said Anna with a shudder. 'You're almost standing on his foot.'

'"Cal's Log",' whispered Mac as if he were in church. They had moved back down the tunnel and were sitting on the floor, their backs to the rock, while Anna slowly and gently turned the pages and Mac held the torch.

'There's a map,' she said.

'He *was* a he,' muttered Mac. 'I tell you I could almost feel him with us towards the end.'

'The end?' asked Anna fiercely. 'It may have been the end for Cal but it's not going to be for us. This map shows an escape route.'

'It could be like the arrows,' Mac warned her. 'I don't think Cal knew where he was going. Just like us.'

'I think we should read the whole journal,' said Anna. 'It's not clear how long Cal was here – or when he made his last entry.' Her voice shook.

They read the log slowly. Soon Mac and Anna had forgotten the danger to their own lives as they shared Cal's sufferings. His story was gripping and they felt a sense of belonging, of sharing his every experience that, in many cases, had been so similar to their own. When they had finished reading both Anna and Mac were close to tears and they sat silently, thinking of the orchard and the plum juice staining the twins' hands and Cal's deep love for his family.

'He still feels he's let his father down.'

'The worst thing is that he was never

found,' said Anna. 'He's lain here all this time without anyone knowing.'

'I expect his family thought Cal was missing, presumed drowned. There might even be a memorial to him somewhere.'

'If we ever get out of here, let's go and look for it. We could trace his family and let them know where he is. Let them know that Cal had mapped what he thought might be a way out.'

She paused. 'What is this possible escape route he didn't have the strength to explore?'

'There's no point in wondering. We just have to get there.'

Mac picked up Cal's map and began to study it carefully. 'We are going to escape, Anna. Cal's going to show us how.'

'I hope he can.' She sounded a little more trusting. 'We need him.'

'He's never been needed more,' said Mac.

'What shall we do about the log? Take it with us?'

'I don't think so,' said Anna. 'I think we should give it back to him.'

'But we have to take the map, Anna.

We'll never be able to remember all the details and won't stand a chance without it. Cal's spent all that time exploring. In the end, he was exploring for us.'

'Yes,' she said, 'you're right. Let's keep the map, but go and give him back his log.'

They went back to the wall and Anna bent down and gently inserted the oilskin package back into Cal's skeletal hand.

'He's lying curled up,' she said. 'Like he was asleep.'

'I think he did just that – like he said. Cal got sleepy, that's all.'

Mac and Anna stood silently for a while, saying their thanks before taking their leave of him. Then Mac took the map and walked slowly back down the tunnel.

What would you have done with Cal's log?

TEN

'The tunnel's going downhill.' Mac swept the walls with the torch beam.

'Let's hope it starts rising up again,' Anna replied. 'Anyway, we don't have any other choice.'

They began to walk, Mac in front this time, Anna following, each preoccupied with their own thoughts. Neither of them had seen anyone dead before, but Cal's bones, although horrifying to discover, had moved them deeply. His death must have been so lonely, so miserable. Had he really just slipped into sleep as they would have liked to think. Or had he suffered? Either way, Cal had died on his own, in the darkness. At least they had each other.

Several tunnels led off the main passage but the arrows on Cal's map firmly indicated that Anna and Mac shouldn't branch off at all. The arrows continued until they were replaced by a single word – HAZARD. Then there was what looked like a smudge.

For a moment Mac and Anna heard a roaring sound and they both came to an abrupt halt.

'What's that?' whispered Mac fearfully.

'I don't know.'

Was it a roaring? Then it came again, only this time it was making more of a rushing, grating noise.

'We're idiots,' said Mac. 'It's the sea.'

Anna felt dazed, as if she hardly knew where she was.

'We've been going down for a long time.' Mac knew he sounded flat.

'When we prayed we might go up. Eventually.'

'I don't think that's going to happen.'

They clambered on, the rocky floor beneath them becoming increasingly rough and full of loose boulders.

Then Mac noticed that one of the tunnel walls was glistening with damp, but he didn't say anything to Anna.

The sound became even more ferocious as they made their way down, until it seemed to fill their ears and block out their thoughts.

Anna was deeply afraid. She could feel the physical presence of the hostile waves as if they were rushing up the tunnel towards her.

Slowly a grey light appeared, and she
knew the sea was there, waiting for them.

They were standing at the mouth of a cave, looking down at the raging current dashing through a channel that had been worn in the rock by years of continuous erosion.

The channel, wide and deep, was filled by the racing tide, travelling at a ferocious rate to the centre of the stack, where it would be funnelled out again through the blow hole.

On the other side of the channel was a wide rocky ledge and the dark entrance to the mouth of another tunnel. Mac shone the torch towards it. 'Looks like that tunnel goes up,' he said, knowing she wouldn't believe him.

For once Anna lost her temper. 'You can't tell. You're just being stupid. Just relying on poor Cal.'

'Thanks.'

'How are we going to get across that channel?' she demanded, still furious with Mac, although she knew she was being unfair. 'You got a plan?'

'No.'

'Then, what do we do?'

'Jump,' Mac replied bleakly.

'*What?*' Anna gazed at him in fury.

'Are you trying to make some kind of joke?'

'No. The only thing we can do is to jump. And we're fit enough to stand a chance – unlike Cal.'

'I'll never make it.' Anna's temper had been wiped out by raw fear, but when she glanced at Mac, she could see that he was just as afraid.

She tried to assess the width of the gap, but it seemed to widen every time she looked at it.

'We'll have to find another way round,' she said at last.

'You know there isn't one. So who's going first?'

'There's no need to do this,' she began.

'We've got no choice,' Mac insisted. 'The stack's almost split in two. Cal explored most parts of this half and couldn't find a way to the top. Now we've got to try the other half.'

'There might not be any way out there either.'

'It's a chance we've got to take.'

'We've taken too many. And the channel's so wide.'

'Shall I go first?'

Anna hesitated, staring down at the

lashing water whose speed was incredible. She knew that if either of them failed to make the other side, they would be swept away and there could be no chance of rescue.

'You've got shorter legs than I have,' she protested.

'So what? It's the run you need.' Mac sounded full of authority but she knew he was making it all up. She wasn't angry with him any more though.

'I'll go first.' Anna tried to pull herself together.

'No. I will.' He sounded stubborn.

'Let's toss for it, then.'

'I haven't got any money.'

'I have. I found 10p in my pocket. Do you want to give it a spin?'

He shrugged. 'If you like.'

Anna dragged out the coin. 'You call.'

'Heads, I go.'

She spun it in the palm of her hand, clasping it for a moment because she couldn't bear to look. Slowly she unclenched her fingers. 'Heads it is,' she said slowly.

'Cal's with you.' Anna spoke softly, trying to conceal her fear. 'He couldn't make it, but he wants us to.'

Mac stared at the foaming water in the channel, which now appeared to be a vast expanse. He must have been crazy to even suggest the jump, let alone attempt it. But he had to do it. And he had to succeed for Anna as much as himself, for it wouldn't be fair to leave Anna alone in this dreadful place. Cal, he said inside. Be with me, Cal. Please be with me.

Do you think both Mac and Anna will make it across the ledge?

ELEVEN

Mac moved back to the tunnel entrance. He then turned round and stared at the raging water in the channel, building up his will power.

Anna felt sick with terror as she waited and watched. Please, God, let him make it.

His eyes wide, Mac began to run as hard as he could, his breath coming in little spurts, his legs pounding. He didn't hesitate as he came to the brink and leapt.

He wasn't going to make it. She *knew* that Mac wasn't going to make it. His legs were too short. His take-off had been wrong. Anna was good at PE. She realized she could have helped him more. Why hadn't she gone first?

Mac made his landing with one foot, but the other still seemed to be dangling in space as if the whole jump was now in slow motion. Then he threw himself sideways and rolled over several times on the slippery, seaweed-hung ledge.

Mac came to a jarring halt with Anna's

cheers echoing in his head, unable to believe that he had succeeded, that he had actually made the impossible jump.

Now it's my turn, thought Anna with a deadly chill running through her entire body. Now I've got to prove myself too.

'If I can jump it, you'll find it easy,' shouted Mac encouragingly, but she wasn't in the least reassured.

Anna's legs were trembling so much that she could hardly move them.

'Go for it!' yelled Mac. 'I'll catch you.'

Her stomach churning and her ears full of the deadly sound of the torrent, Anna ran towards the edge, but soon skidded to a halt. 'I can't do it,' she shouted. 'I'll never be able to do it.'

'Yes, you will. You've got to. You can't leave me on my own. Not to wander around the rest of the stack and then die like Cal. You can't do that to me, Anna!'

She shivered. 'It's no good.'

'Don't be an idiot. When I say jump – you jump.'

'Don't you order me about.'

'Go back. Go back and do it again. Run like crazy. If I can do it – so can you!' he repeated.

Anna turned and went back to the mouth of the tunnel. She gazed at Mac's stocky figure, standing there so bravely, and made up her mind. Somehow she would have to join him.

She began to run as fast as she could, but Anna knew that will-power was more important than speed. That was how Mac had made it and she had to do the same.

'You'll do it. Come *on*!'

Anna was running hard towards the brink, running as she had never run before. She knew that she wanted to stop, that she didn't want to jump, but somehow she had to will herself to carry on, to beat that roaring sound and the horror of the boiling, bubbling, thrashing torrent.

'Come on!' yelled Mac.

Anna could see how terrified he was, how afraid for her and for himself. She couldn't fail and leave him alone.

She could see the edge now, the tide lashing the rock, the huge gap between her and Mac. Help me, Cal, Anna screamed aloud in her mind.

She jumped, her feet scrabbling in mid-air.

Mac grabbed both her arms, and he
and Anna fell sideways in a heap, sliding
dangerously near the edge. But Mac used
his weight to stop them, digging his feet
into mounds of kelp, and they both came
to an abrupt halt.

'We made it,' he yelled, dragging Anna
to her feet. 'We made it!'

She stood beside him. They were both shaking so much that they almost fell.

'Cal was with me. Was he with you?'

Mac nodded. 'But I still didn't think I was going to make it.'

'It's like a miracle we're here.'

'We've got to try that tunnel – go back into the darkness.'

'We've got the torch. It's more than he had,' said Anna. 'But I feel better about it now. We've survived so much.'

'We've got to survive a lot more before we're out,' Mac replied. 'But we're going to make it.'

Suddenly, Anna felt much stronger. She also had the strange feeling that Cal had given them both something in addition to his arrows and his map. Could it have been his will-power?

The darkness swallowed them up immediately, but fortunately Mac had been right. Directly they entered the tunnel they were climbing again, and this time much more sharply than before, leaving the dreadful sound of the tortured sea behind them.

He kept thinking of Cal. If only the

fever hadn't got him. If only he had managed to explore a little further down that last tunnel. Mac was sure that Cal would have successfully jumped the channel. But instead he had died alone in the dark.

Ten minutes later Mac suddenly saw the night sky and came to an abrupt halt. Anna caught up with him and they both gazed up in wonder.

'I don't believe it – the tunnel opens up. It's ending. Coming out at the –'

'Stars,' whispered Anna.

'And there's a bit of moon over there.'

'Where do you think we're heading for?'

'The top of the stack.' Mac gave her a wan smile, knowing that he could easily be wrong.

'Don't get your hopes up,' she replied, pushing past him and beginning to run, stumbling on the rocky floor of the tunnel that just might be leading them into freedom.

But the stack *had* cheated them, and their hopes were immediately shattered. They were on another ledge facing the watery pit once again.

'Wait a minute,' said Anna. She moved towards the edge while Mac shouted at her to be careful.

Looking up, she saw that there had been a rock fall from the almost sheer side of the stack and the debris had built up their side of the ledge. 'We could climb it,' she said.

'Maybe we could even make it to the top of the stack,' said Mac. 'The moonlight's bright.'

'Are we going to do it, then?'

'It's our only chance,' said Mac. 'If we can only get to the top someone will see us. They must be out searching for us.' He paused, suddenly losing confidence. 'You don't think they've given up already, do you?'

'No,' said Anna firmly. 'I don't. And there's something else.'

'What?'

'Cal had a lot of will-power. He has given it to us.'

Anna gingerly sought for a foothold, but the rock below her splintered and gave way, making her slide down the stack, scrabbling and breaking her nails on the rough surface.

'Where are you going?' Mac yelled, terror in his eyes.

'To the top,' Anna gasped, coming to a violent halt as she found hand and footholds at last. 'I'm going to the top of the stack.'

'No one would have guessed it,'

grumbled Mac as he inched his way up. 'You have to feel for every nook and cranny – and then test it first!'

'All right, smarty pants,' shouted Anna.

Soon the climb took on a rhythm, and despite the fact that they were both still terrified of falling, they realized they were making progress.

It was impossible to estimate the distance to the top of the stack, but a bright moon in the cloudless sky bathed them in light and helped them to see where the niches were.

Mac was the first to break the rhythm and to find that exhaustion had suddenly overtaken him, weakening his grip and turning his limbs to putty. He was amazed that this could have happened so quickly and without any warning.

'What's the matter?' she called down suddenly.

'I'm so tired.'

'I don't think it's far.'

'I'm afraid of falling.'

'It's still not that steep,' Anna reminded him.

'It's really hard going. I've got to take a rest. I'll be OK.'

'That could be a mistake. You'll stiffen up. I think there's a bit of a ledge or an overhang just above me. Keep going. You'll do it.'

Mac tried again, and making an enormous effort began to move on.

There was just room for both of them on the overhang, and they lay there panting and wheezing, utterly exhausted.

'You're done in too,' he said eventually.

'I am now. I wasn't then. I didn't think I stood a chance with that jump. This is easier.'

'Not with that pit still below us.'

They were silent for a long time, trying not to look down as they listened to the relentless booming below. How long could they keep going? Would they have to give up? Like Cal.

Then they saw a fountain of coloured light in the night sky.

What is it? wondered Mac. Then he realized they were gazing out at a distress flare.

How had the stack 'cheated' them?

TWELVE

The coloured light lit up the night sky and then gradually faded until only a few specs remained.

'The rescue party are trying to tell us they're still searching,' shouted Anna.

A tremendous sense of urgency filled them both.

'Let's climb,' Mac said. 'They need to see us fast, or they might call off the search.'

He began to scramble up the rock face at once, all his fatigue gone, and soon he was climbing in a frenzy.

'Be careful,' yelled Anna, but she was almost level with him. 'One slip now and you've had it.'

'I just want to make the top. I want to be seen. I think the stack's going to let us go. I think Cal's going to win.'

Mac and Anna reached the top before they realized they were there, and in considerable amazement found themselves on almost flat rock.

At first they could hardly believe in the magnificence of what they saw around them: the familiar coastline; a calm, almost windless sea; and bright moonlight that illuminated half a dozen fishing trawlers and the lifeboat. Their presence made Mac and Anna almost cry with relief and happiness.

Then Mac unzipped his pocket. He took matches out of the plastic holder, and cupping his hands against the breeze that was blowing across the stack, tried to light one of them. But it wouldn't strike.

'Is it wet?' Anna demanded, her anxiety making an unwelcome reappearance.

'It's a dud.'

But with Mac's next effort the match sparked into a flame and he was able to light the flare.

With a sudden whoosh it ignited, spiralling up towards the moon.

Mac and Anna watched the flare light up the sky. Then, almost immediately, they heard the sound of the trawlers' fog horns – a mournful, haunting welcome. They both knew their parents would be out there, and knew how happy they would be.

Yet neither Anna nor Mac could really believe they were safe.

'It seems like we've been on the stack for weeks instead of a few hours,' he said.

'I feel older,' replied Anna. 'We were fools.'

'I know.'

'And we've caused a lot of misery.'

'I know that too,' said Anna. 'If it hadn't been for Cal –'

'We'll repay him. We'll trace his family somehow.' Mac checked he still had the map safely in his pocket. 'He's the real hero.'

The fog horns continued to resound and then they heard a clattering in the air.

'It's a helicopter,' said Anna. 'Air-sea Rescue.'

As the machine hovered above them and a searchlight flooded the dark surface of the stack, Mac and Anna waved desperately, although it was obvious they had been seen.

What do you think Mac and Anna have learnt about themselves?

THIRTEEN

A few days later, when Mac and Anna had fully recovered, they went to their local library to try to find out if there was any record of Cal's ship, the *Petrel*, going down.

The librarian found them a book about wrecks from the local history section and they sat down together at one of the tables to study it. They found the *Petrel* listed, and a strange feeling of sadness and familiarity crept over them as if they had lost an old friend.

The entry read:

PETREL 280 ft Merchantmen
[Patterson-Whitgift Company]
Foundered at Sharp's Stack
Shetland
Lost with all hands
July 17, 1796

'We've got to trace his family.' Mac sounded determined. 'We can start by trying to trace the records of the Patterson-Whitgift Company.'

'I think I can still remember the address that was in Cal's Log – that will help.' Anna suddenly felt confident.

'It'll be a lot of work, but we owe it to Cal.'

'We'll work on it together. I don't care if it takes the rest of our lives.'

'At least we've got our lives,' said Mac.